Ike Goes Golfing

Written & Illustrated by Regina Dahl

WestBow Press books may be ordered through booksellers or by contacting:

WestBow Press
A Division of Thomas Nelson & Zondervan
1663 Liberty Drive
Bloomington, IN 47403
www.westbowpress.com
1 (866) 928-1240

Because of the dynamic nature of the Internet, any web addresses or links contained in this book may have changed since publication and may no longer be valid. The views expressed in this work are solely those of the author and do not necessarily reflect the views of the publisher, and the publisher hereby disclaims any responsibility for them.

Any people depicted in stock imagery provided by Thinkstock are models, and such images are being used for illustrative purposes only.
Certain stock imagery © Thinkstock.

ISBN: 978-1-4908-4614-9 (sc)
ISBN: 978-1-4908-4615-6 (e)

Library of Congress Control Number: 2014914330

Printed in the United States of America.

WestBow Press rev. date: 8/12/2014

WESTBOW
PRESS
A DIVISION OF THOMAS NELSON
& ZONDERVAN

Ike

Goes Golfing

In a cozy, little cabin, deep in Choppenwood Forest, lived a moose named Klondike, or Ike, for short.

Every morning, Ike put on his favorite leather slippers and stretched his moosely stretch before getting ready to start the day.

and wanted to do his very best, so he decided to prepare by exercising his moosely muscles . . .

... making sure that he was in tip-top shape.

Perfect!

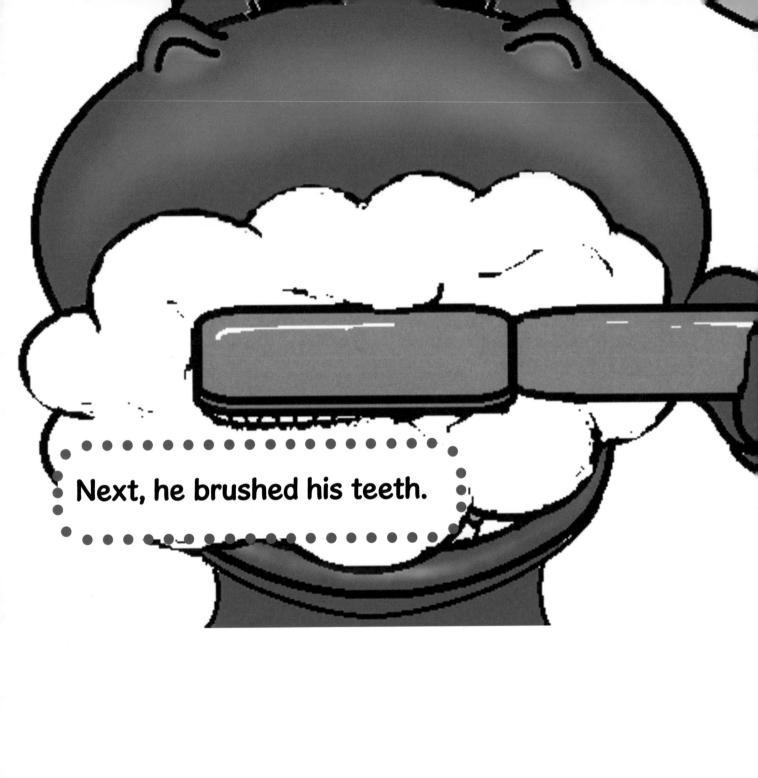

Next, he brushed his teeth.

Then, Ike picked out his clothes, and as quick as a wink, he was dressed and ready for a day on the greens!

Ike packed up his golf gear before he hopped into his bright-yellow jeep, fastened his seatbelt, and headed down the road.

Ike's jeep rumbled up and down the rugged hills and bounced over every bump as he swerved crazily to miss the potholes.

Finally, Ike arrived at the golf course where he traded in his jazzy jeep for a ride that was a little smoother.

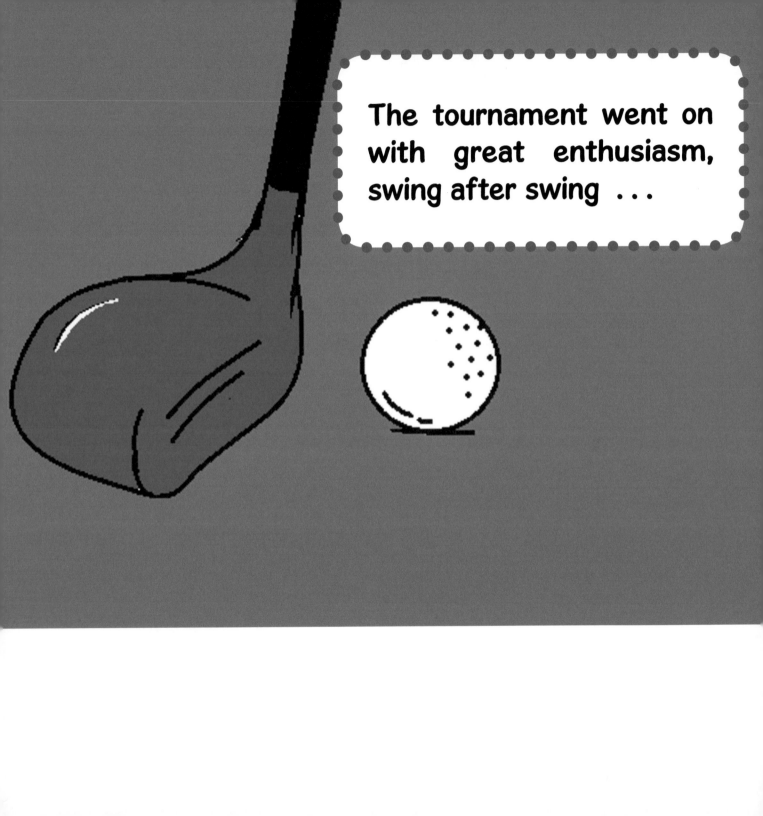

He had to get back to the tournament to give out the awards to the golfers!

As for all four of the little golfers in today's game, each one had lots of fun, as did everybody's official tournament caddie, and a rather good sport himself, Ike. Yes, it had indeed been a terrific day to go golfing.

The End

Printed in the United States
By Bookmasters